RICHARD EGIELSKI

Saint Francis AND THE Wolf

LAURA GERINGER BOOKS

An Imprint of HarperCollins*Publishers*

 First Edition ❖ 1 2 3 4 5 6 7 8 9 10 Library of Congress Cataloging in Publication data is available.

LONG TIME AGO, in Italy, when knights battled and kings and queens lived in grand castles and the rich grew richer and the poor were as poor as ever, there lived a man named Francis.

He himself had been rich once, but God came to him in a dream and told him to give away all his money.

Wherever he went, Francis taught that every man, woman, and child should love all God's creatures that walk on the earth, fly in the sky, and swim in the sea. He could speak the language of animals. And through the miracle of his good works, he became a saint.

One day, Saint Francis came to the rich and busy city of Gubbio only to find the streets empty

and the buildings locked tight.

great wolf, fierce and terrible, had come into the land. The wolf ate sheep and goats, and when there were no more sheep and goats to eat, he ate shepherds. The wolf ate chickens and cows, and when there were no more chickens and cows to eat, he ate farmers.

"his wolf is a terror!" screamed the Contessa di Gubbio. "Something must be done!" She called a town meeting with the town leaders.

"Fear not," they said. "We are sending our bravest knight with the best armor, the sharpest sword, and the strongest lance to kill the wolf."

"Do not kill him," said Saint Francis. "I will go and meet this wolf~"

"Good friar," interrupted the Contessa, "do you expect the wolf to sit down and listen to your sermon?"

"SEND THE KNIGHT!" everyone shouted.

But the knight never returned. So the people of Gubbio went back to the town leaders.

"Fear not," the town leaders said. "Our wealthy city has hired an army to destroy the wolf."

"Brothers and sisters, do not destroy the wolf," pleaded Saint Francis.

"Good friar," said the Contessa, "if we do not destroy the wolf, he will destroy us." Cheering, the people waved the flag of Gubbio as the army marched out of the city.

The army fared no better than the knight. Yet again the town leaders said, "Fear not. Our wealthy city has hired a brilliant engineer to build a great war machine."

"Hah!" cried the Contessa. "Surely a wolf cannot defeat this war machine."

Saint Francis tried to speak, but his voice was muffled by the grinding and clanking of the great machine.

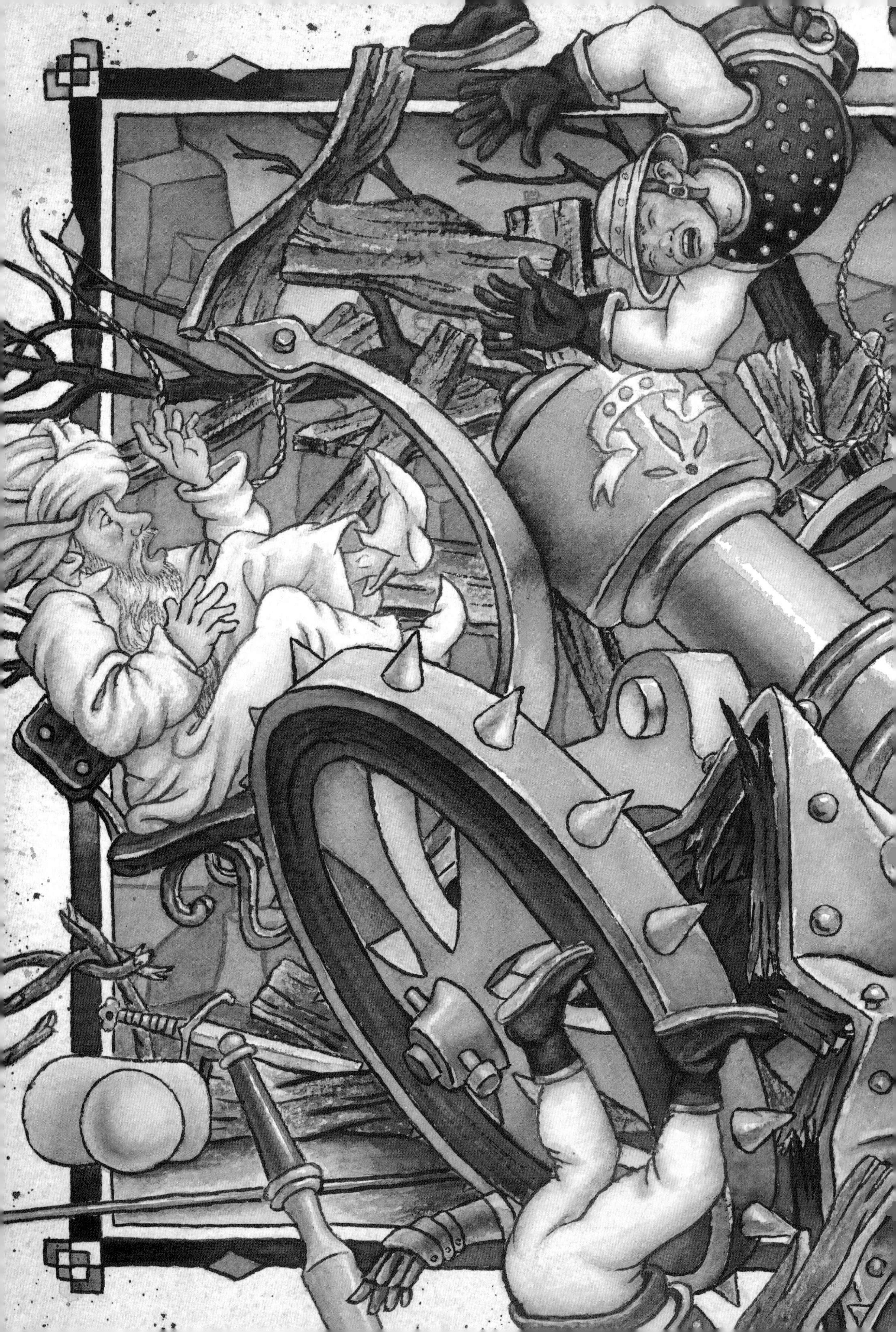

The war machine fared as badly as the knight and the army. The once-rich Gubbio was now poor. The war against the wolf sent the people to bed hungry. Everyone lived in fear.

The Contessa brought the children into her castle to protect and feed them. Seeing the gentle way that Saint Francis comforted them, she was sorry that she had not listened to him all along.

She hurried back to the town leaders. Finally,

they agreed to ask Saint Francis to meet with the wolf.

"Come out, Brother Wolf!" he called calmly in the wolf's own language. "Do not harm me, Brother Wolf, for I love you as I love all God's creatures. I have come to make peace."

The fierce wolf, who ate the knight, scattered the army, and defeated the great war machine, froze before this simple man who spoke of God's love in the language of wolves. He could not resist the friar's gentle understanding.

"Come to Gubbio and make peace," said Saint Francis.

"Do you promise to harm no one ever again?" asked Saint Francis.

The wolf bowed his head.

"Brother Wolf, give me your paw." And the wolf gave his paw.

At the sight of this miracle, the people were filled with great joy and wonder.

Saint Francis said a fond farewell to the wolf and the citizens of Gubbio and left to spread his message of peace and love to others.

From that day on, the wolf wandered peacefully about the city.

He would go to a different house every day for his meals.

After many years, Brother Wolf died of old age.

He was buried in the center of the town square.

The people of Gubbio missed Saint Francis and the wolf. On the anniversary of the day that Saint Francis had come to town, they erected a statue over the wolf's grave.

In Gubbio, Saint Francis and the wolf would always be together. And the miraculous story of how the good friar tamed the wolf with love would live forever.